COMIC CHAPTER BOOKS

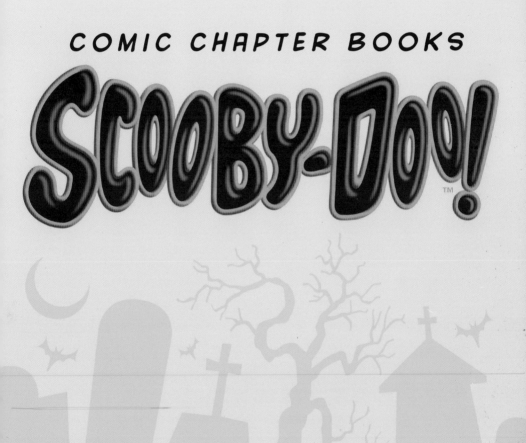

Published by Curious Fox, an imprint of Capstone Global
Library Limited, 264 Banbury Road, Oxford, OX2 7DY
— Registered company number: 6695582

www.curious-fox.com

CAPS37602

Illustrations by Scott Neely
All characters in this publication are fictitious and any
resemblance to real persons, living or dead, is purely
coincidental.

ISBN 978 1 78202 556 6
20 19 18 17 16
10 9 8 7 6 5 4 3 2 1

A CIP catalogue for this book is available from the
British Library.

Summary: Scooby-Doo and Mystery Inc. visit an
archaeological dig, but the camp is deserted. The gang
is convinced that the crew has been kidnapped. Has
the legend of the Gator Man come true, or is it all a big
crock?

COMIC CHAPTER BOOKS

SCOOBY-DOO!

written by Laurie S. Sutton

illustrated by Scott Neely

LEGEND OF THE GATOR MAN

CONTENTS

MEET MYSTERY INC.

SCOOBY-DOO

SKILLS: LOYAL; SUPER SNOUT
BIO: THIS HAPPY-GO-LUCKY HOUND AVOIDS SCARY SITUATIONS AT ALL COSTS, BUT HE'LL DO ANYTHING FOR A SCOOBY SNACK!

SHAGGY ROGERS

SKILLS: LUCKY; HEALTHY APPETITE
BIO: THIS LAID-BACK DUDE WOULD RATHER LOOK FOR GRUB THAN SEARCH FOR CLUES, BUT HE USUALLY FINDS BOTH!

FRED JONES, JR

SKILLS: ATHLETIC; CHARMING
BIO: THE LEADER AND OLDEST MEMBER OF THE GANG. HE'S A GOOD SPORT – AND GOOD AT THEM, TOO!

DAPHNE BLAKE

SKILLS: BRAINS; BEAUTY
BIO: AS A SIXTEEN-YEAR-OLD FASHION QUEEN, DAPHNE SOLVES HER MYSTERIES IN STYLE.

VELMA DINKLEY

SKILLS: CLEVER; HIGHLY INTELLIGENT
BIO: ALTHOUGH SHE'S THE YOUNGEST MEMBER OF MYSTERY INC., VELMA'S AN OLD PRO AT CATCHING CROOKS.

CHAPTER 1
FRIGHT AT FIRST SIGHT

"Ruh-roh!" Scooby-Doo gulped from the back of the Mystery Machine. His eyes grew wide and his mouth dropped open.

"Like, what's wrong, Scoob?" Shaggy asked. The look of alarm on his pal's face sent a wave of panic surging through Shaggy's body.

GRUUMBLE-RUMMMBLE-GURRRRGL!

A strange sound echoed inside the van. Velma, Daphne and Fred were in the front of the Mystery Machine, and they heard it, too.

"What was that?" Velma gasped. She turned around in her seat to look back at Shaggy and Scooby-Doo.

GRRRUMMMBLE-GUUUURGLE!

Scooby-Doo held his paws over his rumbling tummy, but he couldn't hide the weird, rippling movement.

"Zoinks! It looks like there's something alive in there!" Shaggy observed.

"Ri can't help it. R'im hungry!" Scooby-Doo moaned.

Suddenly, Shaggy's stomach growled and gurgled, too.

GRRRUMMMBLE-GUUUURGLE!

"Uh-oh. Your tummy reminded my tummy that it's hungry, too," Shaggy said.

GROOOOAN-GRRRUMBLE!

The two tummies rumbled as if talking to each other.

"But you guys just ate ten minutes ago," Fred pointed out.

Shaggy shrugged. "We can't help it if we digest food fast!"

"You're going to have to wait until we reach Professor Dinkley's camp," Daphne said. "We're almost there."

The kids of Mystery Inc. drove down a rural road on their way to Big Water Lake. Velma's uncle, Professor Cosmo Dinkley, was an archaeologist and had invited them to visit his dig in Florida.

"Uncle Cosmo said he was close to making a big discovery," Velma said. "I wonder what it could be?"

Fred drove the Mystery Machine along a road that was cut through a forest of palms, pines and clumps of palmettos. Large oak trees spread their branches out over the road and dripped with Spanish moss. The thick growth blocked the bright Florida sun, and dark shadows made everything look spooky.

Shaggy and Scooby shivered nervously in the back of the van.

"You two are the only ones I know who can be frightened in broad daylight," Daphne observed.

"We're equal opportunity scaredy-cats," Shaggy replied.

"We're finally here," Fred announced a few minutes later as he drove the Mystery Machine into the Professor's base camp. "But where is everyone else?"

The gang climbed out of the van and looked around. The cabins were empty. Some had their doors standing wide open.

"The camp looks deserted," Fred said, looking around the property.

Daphne noticed an overturned picnic table and chairs. "It looks like everyone left here in a hurry," she said to the others.

"Like, I wonder what happened?" asked Shaggy.

"And where's my Uncle Cosmo?" Velma exclaimed with a gulp.

"It's awfully dark in here. I can't see anything –" Fred started to say and suddenly stopped. He disappeared into the cabin as if he had been grabbed.

"Fred!" Daphne yelped as she saw her friend being swallowed up in the blackness.

"Yaaaa!" Shaggy and Scooby yelled as one.

"It's okay . . ." Fred said weakly from the shadows. "I just tripped."

Daphne pushed open the cabin door the rest of the way and saw Fred stretched out on the floor. He had fallen flat on his face. Daphne helped him to his feet while Velma flipped the light switch. Nothing happened.

"It seems that the power has deserted the place, too. There's no electricity," Velma announced.

Now that they were inside the professor's cabin, the kids looked around at their surroundings. There was a bed, a table and chairs, and a tiny kitchen. Shaggy and Scooby went straight for the miniature fridge.

As soon as they opened it – **WHAM!** – they slammed it shut.

"Zoinks! Velma, are you sure your uncle isn't a professor of biology?" Shaggy gagged. "Like, there's some crazy science experiment growing in there!"

"I guess the electricity has been off for a while," Velma said as she checked out the mouldy wedge of cheese in the fridge.

"Maybe everyone left because the power failed," Daphne suggested.

"Or maybe they left because of the Gator Man!" Fred declared.

"The w-w-what?" Shaggy stammered.

Fred held up an open journal.

"That's Uncle Cosmo's field journal," Velma said. "He uses it to record the daily activities of the excavation."

"It also includes sightings of what he calls the Gator Man," Fred said, pointing to an entry in the journal.

"A creature with the head and tail of an alligator and the body of a man," Daphne read.

"It showed up at the dig site and the base camp," Fred continued.

"This entry says that Uncle Cosmo was worried that the Gator Man was going to scare off the tourists who were helping him on the dig," Velma said. "They were paying him to experience a genuine archaeological excavation. Without them, he can't finance or finish the project."

"Do you think the Gator Man carried off the professor?" Shaggy worried.

"He probably went to the nearest town for help," Fred replied.

"As much as I'd like to search for my uncle, it's getting dark," Velma said. "We should stay here overnight."

Fred agreed. He took Shaggy and Scooby outside to look for some supplies, and they returned a few minutes later.

"Shaggy, Scooby, come on!" Velma said as Fred and Daphne ran after the strange creature.

"Roh way," Scooby said from the safety of the cabin.

"We'll stay here and guard the cabin," Shaggy replied.

"Okay, you can stay here – alone – and hope that the Gator Man doesn't double back," Velma said.

Shaggy and Scooby looked at each other in alarm.

"Rokay," Scooby said. "Ret's ro!"

He and Shaggy followed Velma as she went after Fred and Daphne. The woods were dark and thick with undergrowth. The moon was behind the clouds.

"It was stupid of me to forget a lantern," Velma said. "I can barely see my hand in front of my face."

Shaggy waved his hand in front of his face. "I'm not having any trouble," he said.

"It was just a figure of speech!" Velma said with a sigh.

GRRRROWWLLL!

Suddenly, a strange sound rumbled from a thicket of bushes nearby.

"Like, Scoobs, is that your tummy again?" Shaggy asked.

"Nope," Scooby replied.

"Well, it isn't mine," Shaggy said. He and Scooby looked at Velma.

"It wasn't me!" she exclaimed.

GRRRRROWLLL!

The sound came again, closer this time.

"Ruh-roh!" Scooby gulped.

A large shape came at them through the woods. It stood upright like a human, but it smashed the undergrowth with giant, non-human feet.

"Zoinks! It's the Gator Man!" Shaggy shrieked.

Shaggy, Scooby and Velma turned and ran, trying to catch up with Fred and Daphne. Their legs spun as fast as the wheels of a racing car. They took off at the speed of a Formula One.

The creature was right behind them! The pals zigzagged between the palm trees, trying to confuse the beast. But the Gator Man managed to keep up with them. He made a grab for Scooby's tail. Scooby howled in fright and ran straight up the trunk of a palm tree.

As Scooby peered out from between the fronds, he suddenly felt like he was in an earthquake. The Gator Man shook the tree like a cheerleader's pom-pom. Scooby flew out of the fronds and into the air.

Velma and Shaggy watched Scooby sail through the sky and splash into a lake.

SPLOOSH!

When they got there, they found Scooby doing the doggy paddle towards the shore. Fred and Daphne were nearby, standing where a long trail of reeds had been flattened.

"It looks like this is where the Gator Man escaped into the lake," Fred said.

When Scooby-Doo heard that, he leaped out of the water and landed in Shaggy's arms.

"Let's go back to the cabins," Fred said. "We'll continue our investigation first thing in the morning."

As they left the lakeside, eyes watched them from the water.

CHAPTER 2
TERROR AT THE TIKI

The gang trudged through the thick forest in the dark. They didn't have any lanterns, and thick clouds started to cover the moon. The undergrowth was getting thicker and thicker, too.

"Fred, are you sure the camp is this way?" Daphne asked.

"Um, sure. It's not far. I think," Fred replied. He stopped and looked around.

"I don't know about this, Fred," Velma said.

"We're lost!" Shaggy groaned.

"Re're doomed!" Scooby whimpered.

The clouds gathered overhead and completely blocked out the moonlight. Thunder rumbled not too far away. Fred stuck his finger in his mouth and then held it up in the air.

"How is that going to help us, Fred?" Velma wondered aloud.

"The cabins are on the west side of the lake," Fred replied. "If I can find out which way the wind is blowing, I can use that to guide us."

"But . . ." Velma started to say but was interrupted by a bright flash of lightning and a tremendous burst of thunder.

KA-BOOM!

The kids jumped in surprise. Shaggy leaped into Scooby's paws and hugged his pal.

"Zoinks! That was close!" Shaggy yelped.

The skies opened up, and it started raining. The kids were drenched in a few seconds. Scooby held a palm frond over his head like an umbrella, but it was no use.

"Well, it's not like you weren't already wet from the lake, Scooby," Shaggy reminded his loyal friend.

The gang trudged through the dark, rainy woods. Fierce wind gusts shook the trees around them. Lightning flashes lit up the branches and made the limbs look like claws reaching out to grab them. The clumps of undergrowth looked like crouching creatures in the gloom.

Shaggy and Scooby trembled with every step.

Suddenly, a flare of lightning lit up a hideous face! Its sharp teeth snarled at them from between the trees. The startling sight made even Fred, Velma and Daphne shriek.

"Ahh!" they yelled. The hair on their heads stood up, despite the pouring rain.

Shaggy and Scooby were frozen with fear.

"The G-G-Gator Man! He found us!" Shaggy stammered, just before fainting.

"OOOoooOOoooOh!" Scooby moaned and fainted, too.

Shaggy and Scooby rushed through the door and into the restaurant ahead of Fred, Daphne and Velma. They saw a few customers sitting at tables eating hamburgers and fries, sandwiches and slices of pie. Scooby started to drool with hunger. Shaggy sniffed the yummy aromas drifting in the air.

"Like, I'm in heaven!" Shaggy exclaimed.

"Re, too!" Scooby agreed.

The two pals hurried over to the long counter and plopped themselves down on the stools.

"What'll ya have, fellas?" the waiter asked. He was a thick man with a black moustache and squinty eyes.

"Hamburgers and fries and peanut butter and jam and bologna and cheese with mustard, ketchup and mayo, and a slice of apple pie," Shaggy ordered as he read the entire the menu board from beginning to end.

"Make rat two," Scooby added.

"Comin' right up," the man replied.

When he returned with the food, Shaggy and Scooby-Doo piled up the items in two great big stacks.

CHOMP! CHOMP! GULP!

The pals devoured the meal in a few bites.

Fred, Daphne and Velma came up to the counter and sat next to Shaggy and Scooby. Velma read the name tag on the waiter's uniform.

"Burt, you must be the owner of this establishment," Velma realised.

"Yep," Burt replied. He squinted at the gang as if trying to focus his eyesight. "Say, y'all ain't from around here, are ya?"

"No. We're here to visit my uncle, Professor Cosmo Dinkley," Velma replied. "But his camp is deserted. Have you seen him?"

"Dinkley!" the man grumbled angrily. "That man and his dig have caused me nothin' but trouble!"

"How?" Fred asked.

"As long as he and his archaeology tourists are poking around in the dirt on my property, I can't develop the land. My son and I want to build a hotel and marina over there," Burt said.

"But, if bones or ancient artefacts are found, no construction can be done until the site is excavated," Velma said. "It's a state law."

"Yeah, and we have big plans to build a high-end hotel and swanky marina," Burt said.

"That will never happen and you know it, Burt," a man declared.

The gang watched the man get up from one of the tables and walk over to the counter. He was a large, round fellow wearing a polo shirt and blue trousers.

"My name's Ben Grimmly," he introduced himself to the kids. "Pay no attention to Burt. He doesn't have the money to fix the Tiki Restaurant's leaky roof, let alone the funds to build a multimillion-dollar resort. That's why I've offered to buy the land from him and develop it myself."

Fred chased after the Gator Man into the thick forest.

"Fred! Stop!" Daphne shouted.

"But we've got to help Mr Grimmly," Fred said as he skidded to a halt and looked back at his friends.

"At least let's take some lanterns so we can see where we're going this time," Daphne replied. She took down a lantern that was hanging from the porch rafters.

The rest of the gang grabbed some more lanterns and followed the Gator Man into the woods. It was not hard to follow his tracks. The Gator Man left a trail of trampled undergrowth and giant footprints behind him. There were deep gouge marks in the wet soil made by Mr Grimmly's toes.

"The Gator Man sure made it easy to follow his trail," Fred said.

"Yeah, but I don't like what we'll find at the end of it," Shaggy replied.

GRRRRROWWWLLL!

The menacing sound came from close by and stopped the kids in their tracks. Shaggy and Scooby hugged each other in fear.

"Come on. We've got him now!" Fred shouted.

Suddenly, they heard the sound of something crashing towards them through the woods. Then they heard a terrifying scream.

"Yaaaaa!" the gang shrieked in alarm.

"Yaaaa!" Mr Grimmly yelled as he ran out of the undergrowth and smacked into the kids.

Everyone tumbled over each other in a tangled mess. They formed a ball and rolled back down the trail made by the Gator Man. Just like a snowball, they gathered up broken twigs, leaves and palm fronds as they went. It took the trunk of a palm tree to finally stop them. The ball burst and Grimmly and the gang got tossed in different directions. Scooby landed in a palm tree.

"Ris is familiar," Scooby said as he looked out from the palm fronds.

"Mr Grimmly! Are you all right?" Daphne asked as she helped the man to his feet.

"That . . . that . . . thing!" Grimmly stammered in shock.

"That *thing* is called the Gator Man, and it's been scaring a lot of people around here," Fred explained.

"Well, it sure scared me!" Grimmly shouted. "I'm getting out of here!"

The kids watched Grimmly run back down the trail to the dirt road. They came out of the woods in time to see him get into his car and drive off in a hurry.

CHAPTER 3

CREEPY CREATURE ON THE LOOSE

The kids walked back to the restaurant and found Burt closing up early.

"The Gator Man scared off all my customers," Burt complained. "That monster is bad for business."

"Have you ever seen it before?" Velma asked. "Is it a local legend or anything?"

"Nope. This is the first time I've seen the thing," Burt replied. "It showed up right after that Dinkley guy started digging. Do you think he released some sort of evil spirit?"

"S-s-spirit? Like, a ghost?" Shaggy worried.

"Why not? Big Water Lake used to be native land," Burt revealed. "There are burial grounds all over. That's what Dinkley was digging up."

"Ghosts don't usually drag people into the woods," Velma pointed out.

"What do I know?" Burt snarled. "Now beat it. I'm closing up."

The gang left the restaurant and started to walk back to the cabins.

"Burt Kusiek is not a very pleasant man," Daphne observed.

"He and Mr Grimmly sure don't get along," Velma said.

"It's no wonder. Mr Grimmly is determined to own Burt's land," Fred said. "Did you hear what he said, that he was going to get it one way or another?"

Suddenly, Daphne stopped in her tracks. The rest of the gang almost bumped into her.

"What's wrong?" Velma asked.

"In all the excitement, we forgot to get something to eat at the Tiki Restaurant." Daphne sighed. "There's no food at the camp."

"Let's go back and see if Burt will make some sandwiches for us," Velma suggested.

The gang turned around to return to the restaurant, only to come face-to-face with a frightening figure. The Gator Man!

"Yaaaa!" Shaggy and Scooby yelled.

"Run!" Fred shouted.

All four of Scooby's legs spun like windmills as he sprinted away from the danger. Shaggy grabbed the tip of his tail and was pulled off his feet. He flapped like a flag behind his pal. Fred grabbed Shaggy by an ankle and was yanked off his feet, too. Daphne caught Fred's foot as Scooby fled. She held out her hand to Velma and the whole gang whipped along behind Scooby like the tail of a kite.

When Scooby felt something grab his tail, he thought it was the Gator Man. He didn't look to see if he was right. He ran!

The gruesome Gator Man looked around inside the room but could not see any sign of Shaggy or Scooby-Doo. That was confusing. The Gator Man was sure he had seen them go into this cabin.

The Gator Man lumbered around the living room and then went into the kitchen. He opened the fridge to see if his prey was hiding in there, but got a nose full of stinky cheese instead.

"Gaaaah!" the Gator Man gagged as he slammed shut the fridge door.

The creature stumbled out of the cabin.

When he was gone, Shaggy and Scooby relaxed. Shaggy took the lamp shade off his head and let his spine go slack. He looked around for his pal.

"Scooby-Doo, where are you?" Shaggy wondered aloud.

SPROIIING!

Scooby uncurled himself. He had been all tucked up in a ball to look like a footstool.

"Like, that was close, pal," Shaggy said. "The Gator Man almost got us."

"Ryeah, rat was close," Scooby agreed.

Suddenly, the cabin door burst open with a loud bang!

The Gator Man loomed in the frame of the doorway. He stood between the two pals and freedom.

GRRRRRROWLLL!

"Ruh-roh." Scooby gulped.

"Run for your life!" Shaggy said.

The Gator Man made a grab for the guys, but all he caught was air. Shaggy and Scooby made like baseball players sliding into a base and scooted between the creature's legs.

The Gator Man tried to smack them with his tail but missed and hit the ground.

THWACK!

Shaggy grabbed the doorknob and slammed the door shut – right on the Gator Man's tail!

"Yowww!" the Gator Man howled.

Shaggy and Scooby-Doo leaned up against the door and used their bodies to keep it shut. They could hear the trapped creature crashing around inside the cabin.

CRASH! WHAM! BANG!

"Shaggy! Scooby! What's going on?" Velma asked as she and the rest of the gang ran up to the cabin.

"We caught the Gator Man!" Shaggy replied.

"That's great!" Fred said. "Now we can solve this mystery."

"Or not," Daphne gasped.

The door behind Shaggy and Scooby suddenly opened inwards, and the pals fell backwards. They lay on their backs and looked up at the Gator Man.

"Zoinks! I forgot the door opened from the inside," Shaggy said.

"Run!" Fred yelled.

Shaggy hung on to Scooby-Doo as the pair got dragged across the water by the high-speed motorboat.

FWOOOOOOSH!

The Gator Man twisted the steering wheel of the boat and made it zigzag back and forth. As long as Scooby-Doo's paw was tangled in the rope, he and Shaggy had to follow in the boat's wake.

"Like, I didn't know you could water-ski, Scoob!" Shaggy observed.

"Me reither," Scooby said.

The rest of the Mystery Inc. gang saw their pals being pulled behind the Gator Man's boat and raced to help. Fred pushed the throttle forwards, and their boat sped up to catch the Gator Man.

"Hang on, guys, we're coming to help!" Fred shouted to his friends.

Fred nudged his boat close to the one dragging Shaggy and Scooby-Doo.

The two wakes combined, and the large wave rolled under Scooby.

"Zoinks!" Shaggy exclaimed.

He and Scooby-Doo bounced as if they had hit a giant speed bump. Shaggy lost his grip on Scooby-Doo for a second and was tossed into the air.

Scooby fell backwards and skidded across the water on his back.

When Shaggy came down, he landed on his pal like a surfer on a surfboard. "Like, cowabunga, dude!" he exclaimed.

Fred made a hard turn away from the Gator Man's boat. The wake splashed the Gator Man and almost swamped his boat.

SPA-LOOSH!

The Gator Man let out an evil growl. "GRRRRRRRR!"

Then the Gator Man turned the steering wheel sharply. His boat veered out of control. It headed straight for the shore!

"Ruh-roh!" Scooby exclaimed.

The Gator Man's boat ran aground on the muddy lakeshore. The impact threw the Gator Man into the air.

"ROAARRR!" he screamed.

Shaggy and Scooby went flying, too. The rope around Scooby's back paw loosened and came off.

"Yaaaa!" the two pals yelled as they soared towards the palm trees.

The Gator Man landed in the lake with a big splash.

SPA-LOOSH!

Even though Fred and the others quickly got to the spot where the Gator Man had landed, they could not see any trace of the creature. He had vanished!

"He's gone," Velma concluded, after searching for a moment.

When they got back to the dock, Shaggy and Scooby were waiting for them.

"Let's get back to camp," Fred suggested. "We need to get some rest if we're going to catch the Gator Man tomorrow. I have a plan!"

CHAPTER 4
EERIE ENCOUNTER

The Mystery Inc. gang walked through the forest back to the camp. The cabins were all dark, but Daphne saw a shadowy shape moving inside one of them.

"I think there's something in Professor Dinkley's cabin," she said.

"Zoinks! Not the Gator Man again!" Shaggy worried.

"Rot ragain!" echoed Scooby.

THUMP! BUMP!

They heard the sound of furniture being knocked over.

"Could it be a bear?" Daphne asked.

"Maybe a coyote," said Velma, having read a little about the local wildlife.

"Oww!" came a painful yelp.

"Like, what was that?" cried Shaggy.

"Oww!" the yelp came again.

"It's not something. Someone is in my uncle's cabin," Velma realised.

"Who could it be?" Daphne wondered.

Suddenly, the shape of a round man stumbled out of the cabin door and onto the front porch. He wore safari clothing and a pith helmet. His glasses were crooked on his nose, and he straightened them before he noticed the the Mystery Inc. gang.

"Oh! Hello, kids! There you are!" the man said cheerfully. "Isn't it a little late to be out exploring?"

"Uncle Cosmo!" Velma exclaimed.

"Professor Dinkley! We were worried about you," Fred said.

"Reah rorried," Scooby chimed in.

"Worried? About me? Why?" Professor Dinkley asked.

"Like, we thought the Gator Man had got you," Shaggy replied.

Professor Dinkley chuckled a little at that. "No. I spent all day in town trying to get my archaeology tourists to come back to the dig," he explained. "I'm sorry I wasn't here when you arrived."

"The camp was deserted when we got here," Fred said.

"Rit was rooky," Scooby barked.

"Yeah. Like, what he said," added Shaggy.

"That terrible Gator Man scared away all my clients," Professor Dinkley told the kids. "I've had to refund their money, and without them or the fee they paid, I can't finance or finish the dig."

"We can help you with the dig, Uncle Cosmo," Velma volunteered.

"Like, you're not afraid that the Gator Man will come back and finish what he started?" Shaggy trembled.

Scooby-Doo shook along with him.

"I'm about to make a major discovery at the dig," the professor revealed. "I can't stop now, Gator Man or not."

"Don't worry, Shaggy. I told you, I have a plan to take care of that scaly spook," Fred assured his friend.

"Rut rind of ran?" Scooby asked.

"I'm going to build a trap!" Fred replied. "Once we get to the dig site tomorrow and I study the area, I'll be able to design the perfect ambush."

"And once we have the Gator Man, we'll find out what's behind all his scare tactics," Velma declared.

"Zoinks! Do you mean the Gator Man?" Shaggy gulped.

"The Great Gator Spirit is a guardian of my people," Boone said. "I have performed the rituals and chanted the prayers for him to protect this land."

"Don't you see that I'm trying to learn about the culture of your ancestors, not destroy it?" Professor Dinkley said. He held up the button. "See? I've found evidence that Spanish explorers were here."

"The Spanish destroyed my people," Boone grumbled. "That artefact is a reminder of that terrible time."

"My discovery could bring new knowledge about your people," the professor continued.

Boone wasn't impressed. "You have been warned. Leave this place, or I will have to call upon a more powerful spirit," Boone declared.

Boone turned sharply and walked away. Shaggy and Scooby held on to each other in fear.

"W-what does he mean, 'more powerful spirit'?" Shaggy stammered.

"Oh, he's just saying that to scare you," Professor Dinkley said.

"W-well, he's doing a good job of it!" Shaggy replied.

"Ryeah!" Scooby-Doo agreed.

"Let's not worry about Boone. We have work to do!" the professor declared. "Velma, Daphne, will you help me reset the grid's lines? The storm knocked down some of them. At least, I think it was the storm."

As the girls helped Professor Dinkley restore the grids, Shaggy and Scooby looked around the site nervously, worried that a ghost or a gator spirit might jump out at them from the forest at any moment. They didn't spot a spook, but they did see something sparkly.

"Hey, what's that, Scoob?" Shaggy wondered as he pointed at the glinting object.

"Rit rooks rike a rewel," Scooby said as he used his paws to dig it up.

"Did someone say jewel?" Professor Dinkley exclaimed from the other side of the dig site.

Shaggy pulled the object out of the ground and held it up in the sunlight. He cleaned off the clinging soil. Everyone gasped in surprise.

"It's a ruby!" the professor exclaimed.

"It certainly looks like one," Velma said.

"Do you know what this means, kids?" Dinkley asked excitedly.

"Yeah! Treasure!" Shaggy proclaimed.

"This discovery makes the dig site more important than ever," Professor Dinkley said.

"It also makes it a lot more valuable," Velma observed.

"Maybe the Gator Man is trying to protect the treasure," Shaggy said.

"Or trying to scare people away from it," Daphne replied.

Meanwhile, Fred studied the palm trees growing at the edge of the dig site. He had an idea of how to use them to trap the Gator Man.

When Fred, Shaggy and Scooby were finished building their snare trap, they went over to the other side of the dig site and started to construct a second trap.

"We'll try to drive the Gator Man into the snare trap, but if we can't, this will be our backup," Fred explained. "You can never have too many traps."

The pals gathered the stalks of some palm fronds and stripped the fibres from them. Then they braided the fibres together to form a net.

"Like, are we going fishing?" Shaggy wondered aloud.

"No," Fred replied. "This is part of another type of spring trap. Only this one uses a net instead of a lasso snare."

"Oh! I've seen those in jungle films!" Shaggy exclaimed. "When the explorer steps in it, the net snaps up around him."

"Exactly," Fred confirmed.

"Except in those films, the explorer usually gets captured by cannibals!" Shaggy gulped.

"Don't worry, there aren't any cannibals here," Fred assured his pal.

"Just a big ol' Gator Man with very large teeth," Shaggy shuddered.

Fred finished covering the net with leaves and stepped back from his creation.

"Okay, like, now what?" Shaggy asked.

"We wait," Fred shrugged.

CHAPTER 5
SECRETS REVEALED

Daylight was turning to twilight when Fred finally decided they had waited long enough. The Mystery Inc. gang sat at a folding table under a canvas canopy. It was Professor Dinkley's on-site office.

"I guess the Gator Man is a no-show," Fred sighed. "I don't know if I'm glad or disappointed."

"Maybe the Gator Man is finished trying to scare us away," Daphne suggested.

"That would be a first," Velma said.

"Can we go now?" Shaggy asked. "I feel like a sitting duck out here."

"Reah, ritting rucks!" echoed Scooby-Doo, trembling a little.

"If we're going to leave, we'd better go before it gets dark," Professor Dinkley said. "The road back to the camp is hard to follow at night. We wouldn't want to get lost."

"Like, I'll meet you in the Mystery Machine!" Shaggy proclaimed and jumped to his feet. "Come on, Scoob!"

"Right rehind rou!" barked Scooby, jumping at his chance to leave.

The two pals ran towards the van. They never reached the vehicle.

"Yaaaa!" Shaggy and Scooby shrieked.

Something stood between the two pals and the Mystery Machine. The deep shadows of the tropical Florida forest were spooky even in the daytime.

Now it was nighttime and Shaggy and Scooby saw something that frightened them even more than the dark.

"RAAAAOR!" the thing roared.

"Yaaaa!" Shaggy and Scooby shrieked even louder this time.

Then they backpedalled to get away from the frightening figure. Their legs spun. Their hair stood up straight! They tumbled over each other in a panic and fell to the ground. The creature loomed over them.

"We're doomed!" Shaggy wailed and hugged Scooby-Doo. "Goodbye, Scoobs! You're my best friend!"

"I rove rou, Raggy!" Scooby sobbed.

The two pals shut their eyes and expected the worst. That's why they didn't see their friends rush towards the creepy creature and knock it to the ground.

WHAM!

The kids of Mystery Inc. tackled the monster!

The gang sat on top of the stunned beast, holding him down on the ground.

"Now that's what I call teamwork!" Fred exclaimed.

"You caught the Gator Man!" Professor Dinkley said as he held up a camp lantern to shine on the group.

"Or not," Velma declared as she pulled back the hood of a bearskin cloak and a familiar face was revealed.

"Boone!" the professor exclaimed.

"I dressed as the Great Bear Guardian to protect this place," Boone admitted.

"Did you pretend to be the Great Gator Spirit, too?" Velma asked.

"No!" Boone protested. "The Great Gator Spirit is –"

GRRROWWWL!

Suddenly they heard the low, familiar sound of a gator. Boone smiled as if he had just won a great battle.

Then they heard a tremendous smashing sound.

SMASH! SMASH! SMASH!

"The Great Gator Spirit is right here!" Boone announced.

"Ruh-roh!" Scooby gulped.

The half alligator, half human creature lumbered out of the forest. Its huge feet crushed the palmetto undergrowth. Its tail lashed at everything in its wake. Boone held up his arms to greet the Great Gator Spirit.

"Great Guardian Gator! I welcome you!" Boone exclaimed happily.

The creature paid no attention to Boone. It smacked him aside and headed straight for Mystery Inc.!

GRRROOOOWL

"Zoinks! He sounds really mad!" Shaggy shouted.

"Run!" Fred yelled.

The kids watched the Gator Man sail high over the treetops.

CRAAASH!

SMAHHHHSH!

They heard him land not far away.

"Come on! We can still catch the Gator Man!" Fred declared.

"Wait! Help! Get us down from here!" Shaggy called to his friends.

The gang found Shaggy and Scooby hanging in the net trap. As they freed their friends from the net, Professor Dinkley moaned at the sight of his excavation. The ground was trampled, and the grids were torn up and scattered again. There was no sign of Boone.

"Oh no! Everything is ruined! All my hard work," Dinkley despaired. "Now I'll have to start all – wait a minute. What's that?"

Something shiny poked up out of the churned-up soil. The professor reached down and pulled it from the ground.

"Another ruby!" Dinkley declared. "All that running around must have dug it up by accident."

"Uncle Cosmo! We're going after the Gator Man!" Velma shouted to her uncle as she and her friends stood at the edge of the forest.

"That's nice, Velma. I'm going to stay here and do a little more digging," the professor replied and waved at the kids to go.

The Mystery Inc. gang didn't take long to get to the spot where the Gator Man had landed. It was easy to see where he had come down. There was a big area of smashed undergrowth. But they couldn't find any other sign of him. There was no visible trail.

"How could something so big disappear without a trace?" Daphne wondered.

"Don't worry, Scooby can track the Gator Man!" Shaggy proclaimed.

"How?" Fred asked.

"His nose knows!" Shaggy replied.

"Ryeah!" Scooby agreed.

SNIFF! SNIFF! SNIFF!

Scooby-Doo sniffed the undergrowth that the Gator Man had crushed. Then he pointed with his paw. "He rent rataway!"

Scooby-Doo trotted off into the forest with Shaggy right beside him. They led the way through the thick palmettos. It did not take long for them to reach the end of the trail. The Mystery Inc. gang came to the opening of a large drainage pipe covered with vines and tree branches.

"This is a weird place for a drainage pipe," Velma said.

"What do you mean?" Fred asked.

"I mean, what is it supposed to be draining? There's nothing around here except the forest," Velma pointed out.

"It's a clue!" Daphne said.

"Let's investigate," Fred decided.

The Gator Man slashed at Shaggy and Scooby-Doo with his razor-sharp claws. The pals barely dodged the blows. They jumped into the air to escape, and their legs spun like propellers.

ZZWOOOOSSH!

They took off just like a couple of twin-engine airplanes!

Shaggy and Scooby-Doo zoomed all over the underground warehouse. They bounced off the walls, the floor and the ceiling. At last, Scooby-Doo landed on top of a forklift. He plopped down in the driver's seat, and his foot hit the accelerator.

VROOOM!

The forklift's engine started up without warning.

"Ruh-roh!" Scooby gulped as the forklift sped forwards.

Scooby-Doo tried to drive the forklift, but he was a lousy driver. He crashed into a stack of crates, and then into a pile of boxes.

The contents flew into the air and landed on him with a thud.

Suddenly, Scooby-Doo was wearing fake designer scarves, sunglasses and jewellery. He was wearing so much stuff that he lost control of the forklift.

THUUUUMP!

BUUUMP!

GRRRROWL!

Scooby ran into the Gator Man by accident.

"YOWW!" the creature yelped in pain, but he was not harmed.

The Gator Man held onto the front struts of the machine and roared at Scooby-Doo! The angry growl seemed to make the entire warehouse tremble like an earthquake.

GROWWWLLL!

Now the forklift had no driver and was totally out of control. It veered into another stack of crates.

CRRASSSH!

The crates came down on the Gator Man.

"Scoob! Who knew your bad driving would turn out to be so great?" Shaggy said. He smiled proudly at his pal.

Fred, Velma and Daphne ran up to the dazed Gator Man. They quickly pulled his limp body from the wreckage of the forklift. He couldn't stand but managed to lift his dizzy head.

"Oooooowww!" the fallen creature moaned in pain.

Velma kneeled down next to the Gator Man. She could tell that his face was nothing more than a rubber mask.

"It's time to see if this is a gator or a ghost!" Velma declared as she grabbed the Gator Man's fake snout.

Velma pulled off the Gator Man's mask!

SHLOOOOP!

A familiar face was revealed.

"Burt Kusiek!" the gang gasped.

Kusiek snarled back at them.

"It all makes sense, now," Velma said, adjusting the thick-framed glasses on her nose. "He owns valuable land and he didn't want Ben Grimmly to have it. He pretended to be the Gator Man to scare away Uncle Cosmo and his crew from the dig site because their excavation would have uncovered the secret underground warehouse."

"I was running a smuggling operation to pay for my marina and hotel," Kusiek confessed. "Professor Dinkley and Grimmly were getting too close. I had to scare them away from here somehow."

"But you were in the restaurant when Grimmly was attacked," Fred said.

"My son wore the costume that time," Burt shrugged. "He's stronger than me and could drag Grimmly into the woods. Our plan would have worked if it hadn't been for you meddling kids."

"Another mystery solved!" Shaggy said as he and Scooby slapped a high five.

"Scooby Dooby Doo!" Scooby exclaimed.

BIOGRAPHIES

LAURIE S. SUTTON has read comics since she was a kid. She grew up to become an editor for Marvel, DC Comics, Starblaze and Tekno Comics. She has written *Adam Strange* for DC, *Star Trek: Voyager* for Marvel, plus *Star Trek: Deep Space Nine* and *Witch Hunter* for Malibu Comics. There are long boxes of comics in her wardrobe where there should be clothing and shoes. Laurie has lived all over the world, and currently resides in Florida.

SCOTT NEELY has been a professional illustrator and designer for many years. Since 1999, he's been an official Scooby-Doo and Cartoon Network artist, working on such licensed properties as *Dexter's Laboratory, Johnny Bravo, Courage the Cowardly Dog, Powerpuff Girls* and more. He has also worked on *Pokémon, Mickey Mouse Clubhouse, My Friends Tigger & Pooh, Handy Manny, Strawberry Shortcake, Bratz* and many other popular characters. He lives in a suburb of Philadelphia.

COMIC TERMS

caption words that appear in a box; captions are often used to set the scene

gutter space between panels or pages

motion lines illustrator-created marks that help show movement in art

panel single drawing that has borders around it; each panel is a separate scene on a spread

SFX short for sound effects; sound effects are words used to show sounds that occur in the art of a comic

splash large illustration that often covers a full page or more

spread two side-by-side pages in a comic book

word balloon speech indicator that includes a character's dialogue or thoughts; a word balloon's tail leads to the speaking character's mouth

GLOSSARY

archaeologist scientist who studies how people lived in the past

aroma smell that is usually pleasant

bologna wide, cooked sausage that is cut into thin pieces and eaten in sandwiches

devoured eat something quickly and hungrily

excavation the process of digging up the earth

frond large, divided leaf on a palm tree

menacing dangerous or threatening

native people who originally lived in a certain place

spirit another name for a ghost

tiki decorated in a Polynesian style

VISUAL QUESTIONS

1. Illustrators draw motion lines to help show movement in art. In this panel (page 38), what does the swirling line beneath Scooby-Doo's feet tell you about his action? Can you find other motion lines in this book's comic panels?

2. The way a character's eyes and mouth look, also known as a facial expression, can tell you a lot about how he or she is feeling. In this panel (page 71), how do you think Scooby, Shaggy and Fred are feeling? Use the illustration to explain.

3. In comic books, action often happens in the space between the panels, also known as the gutter. What happens between these two panels from page 57? How do you know?

4. Sound effects, called SFX for short, are a great way to make a comic book panel come to life. List all the sound effects in this book to make your own SFX dictionary!

SCOOBY-DOO JOKES!

What does a skeleton say before every meal?
"Bone appétit!"

How do you unlock a banana?
With a mon-key!

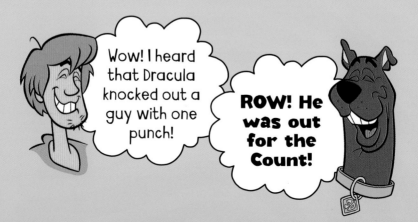

What happens when a banana gets sunburned?
It peels!

Why don't vampires have many friends?

They're such pains in the neck!

Where do ghosts go for treats?
The I-scream parlour!

FIND MORE SCOOBY-DOO JOKES IN...

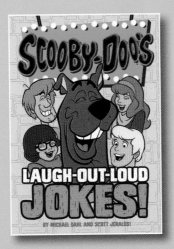

DISCOVER MORE SCOOBY-DOO COMIC CHAPTER BOOKS!

"There's got to be dozens of holes like this," said Velma, looking down at Fred. "Strewn around this side of the mountain."

"I'm just happy it wasn't that deep," said Fred as he finished pushing himself back onto the surface. He hadn't fallen far. The hole he'd discovered in the ground was barely taller than him. With the help of a nearby root and a good jump, Fred had no problem boosting himself right back out again.

"So now can we go?" said Shaggy. "We found another way in. That was the goal, right?"

"But this is obviously not the entrance our 'ghosts' are using," said Fred. "It was completely covered up. You could probably get to the rest of the cave system from there, but no one has used that way for years . . . if ever."

"They're ghosts," said Shaggy. "Since when did ghosts need an entrance, anyway?"

"These do," said Daphne. She was hurrying down the hill towards her friends. "You guys may want to see this."

57

nVelma was looking through the papers on Belastic's desk, I saw a delivery note about a dozen cupcakes to be delivered to his dressing room," explained Velma. "I knew that any place with cupcakes was the most likely place to find you!"

Shaggy flushed. "Like, this was definitely the first place we looked," he said. "And we certainly only ate real food today. Right, Scoob?"

CHOMP! CHOMP! CHOMP! CHOMP!

Scooby wiped icing from his mouth. "Reah," he agreed. "Ro rakeup?"

"What did he say?" asked Daphne.

"Never mind," said Shaggy, embarrassed.

62

Once insi hallway an was small b by the front window. The window looked onto Main Street. But at the moment, it just looked out onto a sea of fog.

Shaggy walked up to the desk and smacked the small bell with his palm.

BRRRING!

Nothing happened.

He looked back at Daphne, who was standing behind him. "Some service, huh?"

"Just be patient, Shaggy," she said.

"Tell that to my stomach," he said, as he turned back around. "Zoinks!" The concierge was standing behind the desk all of the sudden.

"May I help you?" the thin man muttered.

"L-like, we have a reservation?" Shaggy replied. It came out more like a question.

"Of course," the concierge said. He typed something into the computer in front of him.

18

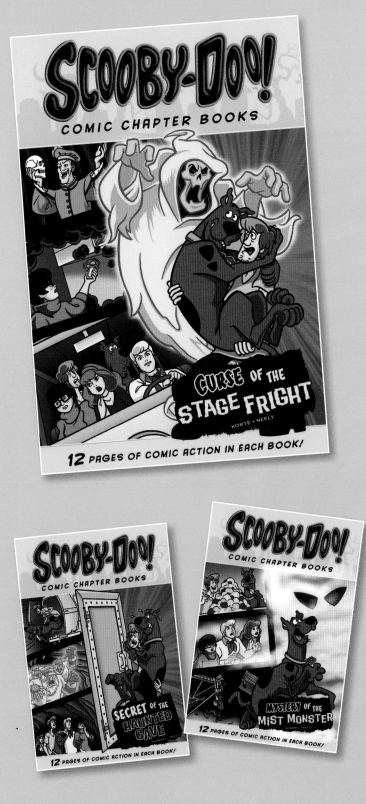

Discover more at

WWW.CURIOUS-FOX.COM